WELCOME TO
PASSPORT TO READING
A beginning reader's ticket to a brand-new world!

Every book in this program is designed to build read-along and read-alone skills, level by level, through engaging and enriching stories. As the reader turns each page, he or she will become more confident with new vocabulary, sight words, and comprehension.

These PASSPORT TO READING levels will help you choose the perfect book for every reader.

READING TOGETHER
Read short words in simple sentence structures together to begin a reader's journey.

READING OUT LOUD
Encourage developing readers to sound out words in more complex stories with simple vocabulary.

READING INDEPENDENTLY
Newly independent readers gain confidence reading more complex sentences with higher word counts.

READY TO READ MORE
Readers prepare for chapter books with fewer illustrations and longer paragraphs.

This book features sight words from the educator-supported Dolch Sight Words List. This encourages the reader to recognize commonly used vocabulary words, increasing reading speed and fluency.

For more information, please visit passporttoreadingbooks.com.

Enjoy the journey!

Little, Brown and Company

Hachette Book Group
1290 Avenue of the Americas, New York, NY 10104
Visit us at lb-kids.com

Little, Brown and Company is a division of Hachette Book Group, Inc.
The Little, Brown name and logo are trademarks of Hachette Book Group, Inc.

The publisher is not responsible for websites (or their content) that are not owned by the publisher.

First Edition: November 2014
Originally published in August 2012 as *New Friends* by Random House Children's Books, a division of Random House, Inc.

New Friends was written by Kitty Richards and illustrated by the Disney Storybook Artists.

Library of Congress Control Number: 2014005322

ISBN 978-0-316-28341-0

10 9 8 7 6 5 4 3 2 1

CW

Printed in the United States of America

Passport to Reading titles are leveled by independent reviewers applying the standards developed by Irene Fountas and Gay Su Pinnell in *Matching Books to Readers: Using Leveled Books in Guided Reading*, Heinemann, 1999.

Disney FAIRIES

Meet Periwinkle

Adapted by Celeste Sisler

LITTLE, BROWN AND COMPANY
New York • Boston

Attention, Disney Fairies fans!
Look for these words when you read
this book. Can you spot them all?

owl

basket

book

snow

Tinker Bell and Fairy Mary
are making baskets.

Each owl takes one basket
to the Winter Woods.
Frost fairies use them
to collect snowflakes.

Warm fairies cannot go

to the Winter Woods.

The cold hurts their wings.

Tinker Bell is curious.

She looks on with Fawn as
the animals get ready to
cross into the Winter Woods.

Tink wants to learn more.
She goes to the library
and takes out a book by
the Keeper.

The next day, Tink
goes to find the Keeper.
The Keeper is in
the Winter Woods.
She hides in a basket
and flies away.

Tink lands in the Winter Woods.

She hides behind the basket.

Her book falls out.

The ruler of the Winter Woods
sees it and gets mad.
"Return this book
to the Keeper," he tells a fairy.
Tink follows the fairy!

The fairy leads Tink
to the Hall of Winter.
The Keeper and
a frost fairy are there.
The frost fairy's name
is Periwinkle.

Their wings start to
sparkle and shine.
Tink and Peri fly
near each other.
The Keeper smiles.

The Keeper takes Tink and Peri

to a special room.

He shows them their past.

The two fairies were born
of the same laugh,
and then it split in two.
Tink and Peri are sisters!

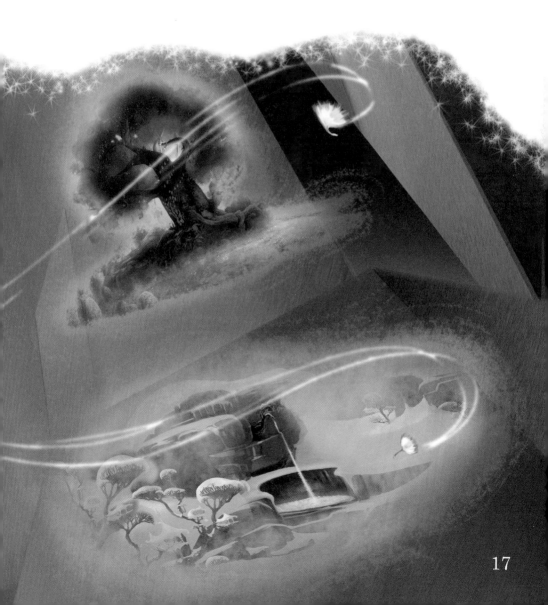

They are so happy!

Periwinkle takes Tink sledding.

She shows Tink her Found Things.

They build a fire
together, too.

Soon, Tink has to go home.

The sisters hug good-bye.

Peri wants to visit Pixie Hollow.

Tink and her friends build a

snow machine.

They hope it will help Peri stay cold.

Bobble and Clank help
Tinker Bell bring the
machine to the border
of Pixie Hollow.
Peri is there.

Periwinkle flies up
to the machine.
Snowflakes encircle
her wings.

The snow machine works.

Peri's wings are safe!

Periwinkle meets all of
Tink's friends and shows
them her frost talent.
It makes the fairies smile.

But soon it gets warmer.

Periwinkle's wings start to fall.

She needs to fly back to

the Winter Woods.

Suddenly, the snow machine
slides into a waterfall.
It gets stuck!

It turns on and
starts making snow.
Pixie Hollow begins
to freeze!

Tinker Bell asks Peri for
help from the frost fairies.
"Their frost can protect the tree,"
Tink explains to Fairy Mary
and the queen.

The frost fairies arrive and
get to work right away.

The frost fairies freeze
the Pixie Dust Tree.
The sun comes out and
melts the frost.
The tree starts making
dust again!

Thanks to Periwinkle
and the frost fairies,
Pixie Hollow is saved!
Everyone is happy.